For my love . . . Chris — A.A.D.

For my sister Cara, who spent time with me in trees — L.R.C.

The Love Letter

Text copyright © 2019 by Anika Aldamuy Denise

Illustrations copyright © 2019 by Lucy Ruth Cummins

All rights reserved. Manufactured in China.

No part of this book may be used or reproduced in any manner whatsoever without written permission except in the case of brief quotations embodied in critical articles and reviews.

For information address HarperCollins Children's Books, a division of HarperCollins Publishers, 195 Broadway, New York, NY 10007.

www.harpercollinschildrens.com

ISBN 978-0-06-274157-8

The artist used Navah Wolfe's old-timey typewriter, gouache, brush marker, colored pencil, and ink wash before finishing the illustrations digitally for this book.

Design by Chelsea C. Donaldson

19 20 21 22 23 SCP 10 9 8 7 6 5 4 3 2 1

❖

First Edition

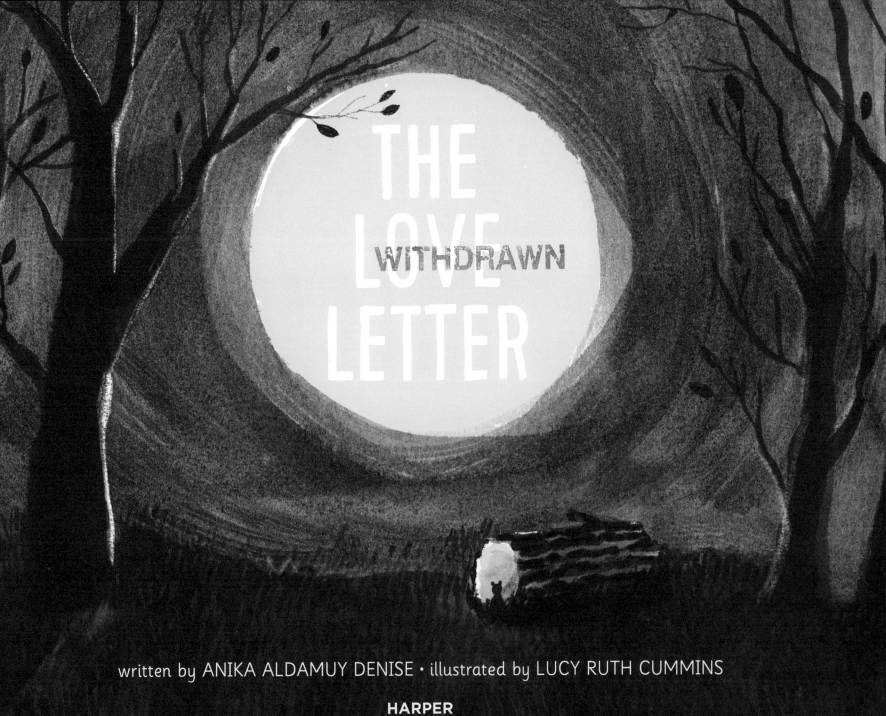

THE LOVE LETTER

written by ANIKA ALDAMUY DENISE · illustrated by LUCY RUTH CUMMINS

HARPER

An Imprint of HarperCollinsPublishers

Hedgehog was late.

He did not like being late.

It further frazzled his already prickly mood.

He'd been grumbling about it to the ground when . . .

he spotted something *unusual*.
It was not an acorn. Or a leaf.
Or any of the ordinary somethings
he came across on his daily walk.
It was a letter.

This wasn't just any letter.

Friend,

You are a joy, a light,

a secret hope,
a safe goodnight . . .
a face that shines just for me.
When you go,
I miss you so.
Don't **you know**
I love you?

It was a
love letter.

"My word," said Hedgehog.

"Someone loves me."

Then he tucked the letter
into his backpack
and went on his way.

Bunny and Squirrel were already in the meadow.

Squirrel was busy gathering acorns, while Bunny busied herself with a nap.

Normally Hedgehog liked to get there first.

But today he had a love letter and was feeling oddly . . . *cheerful*.

When Bunny beat him at leap log?

When Squirrel asked to share his lunch?

And when Bunny wanted a friend to walk her home?

Hedgehog is being oddly cheerful, thought Bunny.

She wasn't in the habit of hugging Hedgehog,
but today she gave him her best bunny squeeze.

She was just about to
hop on home when . . .

she saw a letter
lying on the ground.

Friend,

You are a joy, a light,

a secret hope,

a safe goodnight . . .

a face that shines just for me.

When you go,

I miss you so.

Don't you know

I love you?

"My whiskers,"
whispered Bunny.

"Hedgehog loves me."

Down in the rabbit hole, Mama put her straight to work.
Normally Bunny pretended to nap at chore time, but today
she had a love letter and was feeling oddly . . . *helpful*.

When Mama said peel the parsnips?

Perfect!

When Sister said set the table?

Surely!

And when Papa
said sweep the floor?

Splendid!

After supper, she hopped
along to Squirrel's house.

"I brought you more acorns,"
said Bunny.
Bunny is being oddly helpful,
thought Squirrel.

Before he could say *Thanks a bundle,*
Bunny overturned her apronful
of acorns onto the pile.

Squirrel's neatly stacked acorns came
tumbling down!

"Bunny should be less of a busy-bunny."
Squirrel sighed.
Then he spotted something
unusual among the acorn scatter.

It was a letter.

Friend,

You are a joy, a light,

a secret hope,

a safe goodnight . . .

a face that shines just for me.

When you go,

I miss you so.

Don't you know

I love you?

"Aww, nuts," said Squirrel. "Bunny loves me."

Normally messiness
made Squirrel anxious.

But today he had a love letter
and was feeling oddly . . . *carefree.*

When Mama splashed soup on his napkin?

Slurp!

When Papa left wood shavings on the floor?

Scoop!

When Squirrel's teddy bears were not in size order?

Snooooore!

The next morning, Hedgehog, Bunny, and Squirrel
bundled up and headed to the meadow.
"If I do not show, Bunny will miss me so," said Squirrel.

"If I do not show, Hedgehog will
miss me so," said Bunny.

"If I do not show, I might never know who sent me this love letter," said Hedgehog.

No one said a word at first.

The letter that had made Hedgehog cheerful and Bunny helpful
and Squirrel carefree suddenly made them all . . . shy.

Squirrel gathered the courage
to speak first.
"Bunny," he said, pulling
the love letter from his pocket,
"I may not have your gift for
words, but—"

"My letter!" said Bunny, snatching it up.

"My letter!" cried Squirrel, grabbing it back.

"My letter!" insisted Hedgehog, stealing it away.

And on it went: snatch, grab, steal, bicker. Until—

"Look what you've done,"
said Bunny.

"You ripped it,"
said Squirrel.

"Did not!"

"Did too!"

"Did NOT!"

"Excuse me."

"Was that my letter?" asked Mouse.

"Your letter?" said Hedgehog. "I'm not sure.
What did it say?"

Friend,

You are a joy, a light,

a secret hope,

a safe goodnight . . .

a face that shines   just for   me.

When you go,

I miss you so.

Don't you   know

I love you?

"You wrote the letter?" said Bunny. "But who is it for?"

"The moon,"

said Mouse.

"Why does the moon need a love letter?" asked Hedgehog.

"Because I'm a small mouse in a dark forest,
and the moon is my very good friend.
Don't you have a very good friend?"

Hedgehog, Bunny, and Squirrel looked from one to the other.

They *were* good friends.

Friends who shared their lunch.

And walked each other home.

And gave hugs.

And brought acorns.

"This was all a terrible mix-up," said Hedgehog.

"The love letter never really belonged to any of us," added Bunny.

"We shouldn't be arguing over something we never had." Squirrel sighed.

Mouse looked at their long faces.

"When you thought the letter was for you—how did you feel?" she asked.

"Cheerful,"
said Hedgehog.

"Helpful,"
said Bunny.

"Carefree,"
said Squirrel.

"And . . . ?" asked Mouse.

"Loved."

"Then I'd call that a *wonderful* mix-up!" said Mouse.